Critter County ®

# THE GREAT BALLOON ADVENTURE

Paula Bussard
Illustrated by Yakovetic

Chariot Books™
David C. Cook Publishing Co.

Dedicated to
Jaime and Ryan Wyrtzen
Christa and Jonathan Bussard
Whitney and Kristin Hesser
Thank you for showing us the eternal value of a child's heart. And
for reminding us of a child's swiftness to trust the God who tells
us to maintain that kind of simple faith.

Chariot Books™ is an imprint of David C. Cook Publishing Co.

David C. Cook Publishing Co., Elgin, Illinois 60120
David C. Cook Publishing Co., Weston, Ontario

THE GREAT BALLOON ADVENTURE
©1989 by Loveland Communications for text and illustrations

Book design by Stephen D. Smith
First Printing, 1989

Printed in the United States of America
94  93  92  91  90  89   5  4  3  2  1

Bussard, Paula J.
    The great balloon adventure.
    (Critter County)
    Summary: Piloting a hot air balloon with all the critters on board, Lester loses his way
and his confidence until Christine recites verses from the Book of Proverbs and reminds
Lester that loving God restores one's confidence.
    [1. Confidence–Fiction. 2. Hot air balloons–Fiction. 3. Balloon ascensions–Fiction. 4.
Animals–Fiction. 5. Christian life–Fiction] I. Yakovetic, ill. II. Title. III. Series: Bussard,
Paula J. Critter County books.
PZ7.B9658Gt 1989          [E]          89-22078

ISBN 1-55513-900-0

All Scripture quotations in this publication are from the Holy Bible, New International
Version. Copyright ©1973, 1978, 1984, International Bible Society.

Lester loaded the last piece of luggage and raised his hand into the air. "Oh, my stars, we are ready to lift off at last. The skies are calling, my adventurous friends. Let us set sail!" he exclaimed.

"Everyone in. Next stop—Christine's house!" added Sydney. "We'll have one *great* party!"

As the balloon rose gently into the morning sunshine, all the Critter County critters cheered. It was a perfect day for a flight. Lester smiled from ear to ear. Flying this balloon was his dream come true.

Nothing could spoil *this* trip. Well . . . almost nothing.

Suddenly the wind began to blow, bringing a dark fog with it. A few raindrops quickly became a downpour.

"Oh, Mr. Lester!" Motorboat cried. "If I'd wanted to get wet, I'd have revved up my little beaver tail and swum to Christine's!"

"Yeah, Lester. My tail is soaked, my sneakers are squishy, and even my ear lobes are shivering!" Rascal complained.

Poor Lester got so nervous he began to chew on his tail. *"Oh, me, oh, my,"* he thought. *"Is it true? Can this be? Am I really . . . lost?"*

The balloon bounced through the windy storm. As the critters slid from side to side, they started asking questions that poor old Lester couldn't answer.

"*When* are we going to get to Christine's party?" asked Motorboat.

"Yeah, Lester, where are we, anyway?" Rascal chimed in.

Sydney interrupted. "Now, now. Lester's doing a good job of navigating this ship. We'll get there."

"Thanks for believing in my vast piloting experience and expertise, Sydney," Lester said.

"To be honest, Lester, I am a bit concerned," Sydney whispered. "Christine was expecting us to arrive over an hour ago. Just when *do* you think we'll get there?"

"Um, let's see. I'm sure her house is just over this ridge, or just beyond that little creek . . . or maybe, it's over there by that . . ." Lester stopped and took a deep breath. "Well, shudder in my shoes, Sydney. Suppose I can't find it?"

"Now, Lester, I just know you'll get us there. Hang on to your confidence. Nobody can take it from you, unless you give it to them," Sydney said, trying to reassure Lester.

But Rascal interrupted. "I'd have confidence if Lester had a map."

"My dear boy, 'tis the *only* thing I forgot. Besides, who needs a map? . . . Oh, if only the fog would lift," Lester went on. "Oh, Christine, Christine. . . . Wherefore art thou, my Christine?"

Just then Lester's wife, Liona Lou, yelled, "Lester, Lester! Did you pack my overnight case? I can't seem to find it."

"Liona, my little petunia, this is a hot air balloon, not a 747," Lester reminded her. "There wasn't room for it."

Liona threw up her hands and wailed, "Oh, what will I do? How will I ever brush my tail?"

Lester's lip began to quiver. The raindrops mixed with the tears on his cheeks. He felt as though he couldn't do anything right. Suddenly he perked up and shouted, "Aha! The fog is lifting!"

All the critters cheered as first they saw some apple trees and then, a little house nestled in the hills. Was music coming from the house?

"Oh, Christine, can you hear us? We're coming . . . we've landed!"

"Hey, kids! Hurry, they're here!" Christine called, running outside. "How was your trip?" she asked.

Well, that was the wrong thing to ask! Everyone started moaning and groaning and complaining. Everyone but Lester. He looked tired and sad, especially when Motorboat said, "Mr. Lester told us he could *fly* that balloon."

Finally Lester spoke. "Oh, Christine, what a day I have had!"

"I am so sorry, Lester. The good news is that you're here safe and sound," Christine assured him.

As the children joined Christine, the critters (except for Lester) forgot about their terrible trip. They were so glad to see their good friends. Sydney spotted Christa. "How's school?" he asked her.

"It's okay except for math. I'll never understand it!" she told him.

"Hey, where's your confidence, Christa?" Sydney asked.

"But, Sydney," she answered. "I have to work so hard at math."

"Hard work is the price we pay to travel the road of success," Sydney answered cheerfully. "Just keep at it. You'll make it."

Soon everyone was in the living room munching on snacks and playing music. But Jaime was worried. "Mom, nobody mentioned the cookies I baked. I bet they're awful."

"My, we do have a 'confidence crisis' around here. Honey, you've baked those cookies six or eight times before. They're always wonderful," Christine said reassuringly.

"Hey, Christine. Great chocolate chip cookies!" Sydney interrupted. "They're the best I've ever had."

"Thanks, Sydney, but I can't take any credit. Jaime deserves the pat on the back."

Jaime smiled. "Well, Mom, guess you were right again."

Christine looked at the happy group. She said, "I was thinking that with all these struggles over having confidence, we need to remember our 'Proverbs Promises.'"

"What's confidence?" Kristin asked, climbing on Christine's lap.

"Confidence is the feeling we have when we learn how much God loves us and we choose to walk with Him for the rest of our lives," Christine explained. "We know He's always with us, and will help us, no matter what happens. But before we can walk anywhere, we have to learn which paths to take. So we made up a game to help us learn Bible verses that will help us walk in God's paths.

"Come on, guys, here's the first song," she added.

As Christine and the critters played the first four notes, Christa yelled, "I've got it! Proverbs 2:20. 'Walk in the ways of good men and keep to the paths of the righteous.'"

"Great!" Christine cheered. "We can have confidence when we know we're following the right kind of people."

When Jaime heard the next notes she said, "That's Proverbs 4:27. 'Do not swerve to the right or the left. Keep your foot from evil.'"

Ryan quickly said, "I get to go next." But when the song began, he hesitated. Finally he said, "It's about integrity, but I don't think I can say it all. It's too hard."

"Put on your thinking cap. I know you'll get it," Sydney encouraged him.

"'The man of integrity walks,'" he started. "Uh, umm, 'walks securely; but he who takes crooked paths will be found out.' Proverbs 10:9."

As the critters and kids cheered him on, Whitney asked, "What does integrity mean?"

"Sounds like a new flavor of iced tea, if you ask me," Liona Lou answered.

Sydney laughed. "Sounds good, doesn't it, Liona Lou? Well, Whitney, *integrity* means being honest. It means that you always tell the truth so that people can depend on what you say."

The game ended when Jonathan knew Proverbs 3:5, 6: "Trust in the Lord with all your heart and lean not on your own understanding; in all your ways acknowledge him and he will make your paths straight."

As Christine went to get dinner, she found Lester sitting in the laundry room. "I'm a bundle of nerves. I am most truly . . . a basket case. It's the flight home," he explained. "How will I do it? They're all depending on me. If they had any ideas of the flock of butterflies currently flapping their wings in my stomach."

"Now, Lester, remember how you prepared for this trip. You made it once. I'm sure you can find your way back to Critter County. "

"Oh, Christine, do you mean it? Do you really think I can do it?" Lester exclaimed.

"Of course you can, Lester. Your only problem is your sagging confidence."

"Well, if that's all that's wrong with me—I'll just tighten my belt. Oh, Christine, my lovely rosebud, I thank you from the depths of my heart. You have restored my vision, renewed my faith, rebuilt my confidence. Yes, together we can—"

"Together we can finish dinner!" Christine said with a smile.

After a big dinner, more games and songs, and a lot of laughter, the critters headed out to their balloon.

Jaime and Christa walked with Sydney, who was carrying a bag of chocolate chip cookies. He turned to Christa and said, "I know you'll learn that math."

"Yeah, I probably will," she answered. "I'll just have to keep studying."

Christine smiled. "I do believe our confidence is growing. Christa will keep studying, and Jaime will keep practicing her baking. As we all do our best we can face whatever happens because we know God loves us and will be walking with us."

Before the critters climbed in their balloon, everyone had gifts for them—mittens and blankets in case they were stranded over the North Pole, bug spray if they landed in the jungle, and—just in case—a map!

As they took off, Lester called back, "This is one small step for a lion, one giant leap for Critter County...."

The last thing Christine and the kids saw as the balloon rose over the trees was the map, fluttering to earth.

"Do you think we'll ever hear from them again, Mom?" Ryan asked.

"Yes, Ryan, they'll find their way back to Critter County. Lester has his confidence back," Christine answered. "And I have confidence in him, too!"

If Lester's story has helped your confidence grow, please write and tell him. It will be an encouragement to him. Write to:

Lester
Critter County
Box 8
Loveland, OH 45140